HOCUS POCUS DIPLODOCUS

The World's First-Ever Magician

For Isaac and Niamh

Written by **Steve Howson**   Illustrated by **Kate Daubney**

One hundred and fifty million years ago, Hocus P. Diplodocus was born.

From the moment he hatched out of his egg, Hocus was different...

He let out a little sneeze and his eggshell disappeared with a loud POP.

"How strange," thought his mummy.
But she was hungry, and diplodocuses have very small brains.
So she went to eat some leaves and forgot all about it.

Hocus discovered he could do lots of unusual things that the other dinosaurs could not.

With a flick of his tail he could make fruits, rocks and even other dinosaurs disappear.

Then, he could make them
reappear, often a long way away...

...which some of his friends
found very annoying.

Hocus could produce a flock of pterodactyls out of thin air.

He felt sure he could slice
another dinosaur in half and then
put them back together again.

But nobody would let him try.

Sometimes, Hocus made things disappear by accident.

Once, he was about to tuck into a big bush of his favourite juicy leaves, when a fly buzzed right up his nose.

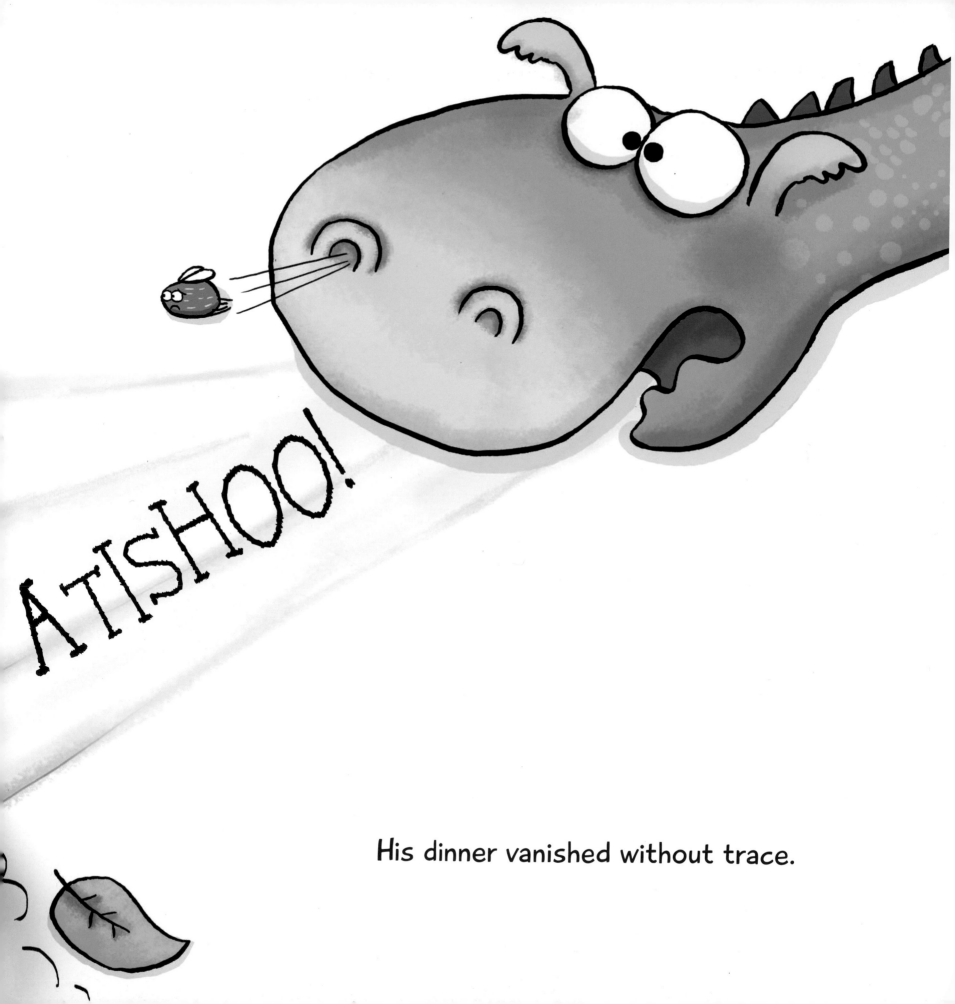

ATISHOO!

His dinner vanished without trace.

Then one day...

GGRROARR

...a hungry Tyrannosaurus Rex leapt out of the forest, taking Hocus and his friends by surprise.

It was just about to snap its jaws around Burpy Barosaurus's neck, when Hocus flicked his tail...

...and made all of its teeth fall out.

The T. rex dropped Burpy into a pool of dribble and fled.

"Hooray!" cheered all the little dinosaurs.
Burpy let out a huge sigh of relief - and a small burp.

"That was amazing!" cried Stevie Stegosaurus.

"You should put on a show," said Ian Iguanodon, "but we'll need to call you something special."

"Great idea!" said Hocus. "We could use that 'P' in the middle of my name."

"How about Penelope?"
said Terry Triceratops, with a grin.

"Pimplebottom,"
said Burpy, who couldn't
stop giggling.

"Ptimmy," said Pteresa Pteranodon.

"I've got it," cried Ian Iguanodon. "POCUS!"

Dinosaurs came from all over the swamp to see Hocus Pocus Diplodocus perform the world's first magic show.

Nobody had ever seen anything like it.

For his birthday, Hocus Pocus Diplodocus
decided to put on the biggest magic show ever.
Thousands of dinosaurs came to watch.

Hocus began to summon all of his powers.

He felt a tingling from the top of his nose to the tip of his tail.

But then, the tingling in his nose turned into a tickle.

Hocus wriggled his nose to try and stop it, but that just made it worse...

There was a huge flash of light,
and all the dinosaurs disappeared...

To this day, nobody really
knows where they went.

Do you?

Hocus Pocus Diplodocus
An original concept by author Steve Howson
© Steve Howson
Illustrated by Kate Daubney

Published by MAVERICK ARTS PUBLISHING LTD
Studio 3A, City Business Centre, 6 Brighton Road, Horsham, West Sussex, RH13 5BB
© Maverick Arts Publishing Limited May 2014 +44 (0)1403 256941

ISBN 978-1-84886-112-1

Maverick
arts publishing
www.maverickbooks.co.uk